Flower Fairies of the Autumn

with the nuts and berries they bring

POEMS AND PICTURES BY

CICELY MARY BARKER

BLACKIE: LONDON AND GLASGOW

THE BERRY-QUEEN

An elfin rout,
  With berries laden,
Throngs round about
  A merry maiden.

Red–gold her gown;
  Sun-tanned is she;
She wears a crown
  Of bryony.

The sweet Spring came,
  And lovely Summer:
Guess, then, her name—
  This latest-comer!

Distributed in the United States by
Two Continents Publishing Group Ltd.,
30 East 42nd Street, New York, NY 10017

Blackie & Son Ltd., Bishopbriggs, Glasgow
450 Edgware Road, London W2 1EG

Printed in Great Britain by Smith and Ritchie Ltd., Edinburgh.

CONTENTS

THE SONG OF
THE MOUNTAIN ASH FAIRY

They thought me, once, a magic tree
   Of wonderous lucky charm,
And at the door they planted me
   To keep the house from harm.

They have no fear of witchcraft now,
   Yet here am I to-day;
I've hung my berries from the bough,
   And merrily I say:

" Come, all you blackbirds, bring your wives,
   Your sons and daughters too,
The finest banquet of your lives
   Is here prepared for you."

(The Mountain Ash's other name is Rowan; and it used to be called Witchentree and Witch-wood too.)

The Mountain Ash Fairy

THE SONG OF
THE LORDS-AND-LADIES FAIRY

Fairies, when you lose your way,
   From the dance returning,
In the darkest undergrowth
   See my candles burning!
These shall make the pathway plain.
Homeward to your beds again.

(These are the berries of the Wild Arum, which has many other
names, and has a flower like a hood in the Spring. The berries
are not to be eaten; please do not eat anything in this book
except those which say that you may; they may be good for
birds but not for boys and girls.)

The Lords-and-Ladies Fairy

THE SONG OF
THE WAYFARING TREE FAIRY

My shoots are tipped with buds as dusty-
  grey
As ancient pilgrims toiling on their way.

Like Thursday's child with far to go, I
  stand,
All ready for the road to Fairyland;

With hood, and bag, and shoes, my name
  to suit,
And in my hand my gorgeous-tinted fruit.

The Wayfaring Tree Fairy

THE SONG OF
THE ROBIN'S PINCUSHION FAIRY

People come and look at me,
Asking who this rogue may be?
—Up to mischief, they suppose,
Perched upon the briar-rose.

I am nothing else at all
But a fuzzy-wuzzy ball,
Like a little bunch of flame;
I will tell you how I came:

First there came a naughty fly,
Pricked the rose, and made her cry;
Out I popped to see about it;
This is true, so do not doubt it!

The Robin's Pincushion Fairy

THE SONG OF
THE ELDERBERRY FAIRY

Tread quietly:
O people, hush!
—For don't you see
A spotted thrush,
One thrush or two,
Or even three,
In every laden elder-tree?

They pull and lug,
They flap and push,
They peck and tug
To strip the bush;
They have forsaken
Snail and slug;
Unseen I watch them, safe and snug!

(These berries do us no harm, though they don't taste very nice.
Country people make wine from them; and boys make
whistles from elder stems.)

The Elderberry Fairy

THE SONG OF
THE BURDOCK FAIRY

Wee little hooks on each brown little bur,
(Mind where you're going, O Madam and
    Sir!)
How they will cling to your skirt-hem and
    stocking!
Hear how the Burdock is laughing and
    mocking:
Try to get rid of me, try as you will,
Shake me and scold me, I'll stick to you
    still,
       I'll stick to you still!

The Burdock Fairy

THE SONG OF
THE ACORN FAIRY

To English folk the mighty oak
  Is England's noblest tree;
Its hard-grained wood is strong and good
  As English hearts can be.
And would you know how oak-trees
    grow,
  The secret may be told:
You do but need to plant for seed
  One acorn in the mould;
For even so, long years ago,
  Were born the oaks of old.

The Acorn Fairy

THE SONG OF THE DOGWOOD FAIRY

I was a warrior,
  When, long ago,
Arrows of Dogwood
  Flew from the bow.
Passers-by, nowadays,
  Go up and down,
Not one remembering
  My old renown.
Yet when the Autumn sun
  Colours the trees,
Should you come seeking me,
  Know me by these:
Bronze leaves and crimson leaves,
  Soon to be shed;
Dark little berries,
  On stalks turning red.

(Cornel is another name for Dogwood; and Dogwood has
nothing to do with dogs. It used to be Dag-wood, or Dagger-
wood, which, with another name, Prickwood, show that it
was used to make sharp-pointed things.)

The Dogwood Fairy

THE SONG OF
THE BLACK BRYONY FAIRY

Bright and wild and beautiful
For the Autumn festival,
I will hang from tree to tree
Wreaths and ropes of Bryony,
To the glory and the praise
Of the sweet September days.

(There is nothing black to be seen about this Bryony, but
people do say it has a black root; and this may be true, but you
would need to dig it up to find out. It used to be thought a cure
for freckles.)

The Black Bryony Fairy

THE SONG OF
THE HORSE CHESTNUT FAIRY

My conkers, they are shiny things,
    And things of mighty joy,
And they are like the wealth of kings
    To every little boy;
I see the upturned face of each
    Who stands around the tree:
He sees his treasure out of reach,
    But does not notice *me*.

For love of conkers bright and brown,
    He pelts the tree all day;
With stones and sticks he knocks them
    down,
    And thinks it jolly play.
But sometimes I, the elf, am hit
    Until I'm black and blue:
O laddies, only wait a bit,
    I'll shake them down to you!

The Horse Chestnut Fairy

THE SONG OF
THE BLACKBERRY FAIRY

My berries cluster black and thick
For rich and poor alike to pick.

I'll tear your dress, and cling, and tease,
And scratch your hands and arms and
    knees.

I'll stain your fingers and your face,
And then I'll laugh at your disgrace.

But when the bramble-jelly's made,
You'll find your trouble well repaid.

(Here is something you may eat!)

The Blackberry Fairy

THE SONG OF
THE NIGHTSHADE BERRY FAIRY

" You see my berries, how they gleam and
      glow,
Clear ruby-red, and green, and orange-
      yellow;
Do they not tempt you, fairies, dangling so?"
   The fairies shake their heads and answer " No!
     You are a crafty fellow!"

" What, won't you try them? There is
      naught to pay!
Why should you think my berries poisoned
      things?
You fairies may look scared and fly away—
The children will believe me when I say
      My fruit is for kings!"
  But all good fairies cry in anxious haste,
   " *O children, do not taste!*"

(You must believe the good fairies, though the berries look
nice. This is the Woody Nightshade, which has purple and
yellow flowers in the summer.)

The Nightshade Berry Fairy

THE SONG OF
THE ROSE HIP FAIRY

Cool dewy morning,
  Blue sky at noon,
White mist at evening,
  And large yellow moon;

Blackberries juicy
  For staining of lips;
And scarlet, O scarlet
  The Wild Rose Hips!

Gay as a gipsy
  All Autumn long,
Here on the hedge-top
  This is my song.

The Rose Hip Fairy

THE SONG OF THE YEW FAIRY

Here, on the dark and solemn Yew,
    A marvel may be seen,
Where waxen berries, pink and new,
    Appear amid the green.

I sit a-dreaming in the tree,
    So old and yet so new;
One hundred years, or two, or three
    Are little to the Yew.

I think of bygone centuries,
    And seem to see anew
The archers face their enemies
    With bended bows of Yew.

The Yew Fairy

THE SONG OF
THE CRAB-APPLE FAIRY

Crab-apples, Crab-apples, out in the wood,
Little and bitter, yet little and good!
The apples in orchards, so rosy and fine,
Are children of wild little apples like mine.

The branches are laden, and droop to the
    ground;
The fairy-fruit falls in a circle around;
Now all you good children, come gather them
    up:
They'll make you sweet jelly to spread when
    you sup.

One little apple I'll catch for myself;
I'll stew it, and strain it, to store on a shelf
In four or five acorn-cups, locked with a key
In a cupboard of mine at the root of the tree.

THE SONG OF
THE SPINDLE BERRY FAIRY

See the rosy-berried Spindle
All to sunset colours turning,
Till the thicket seems to kindle,
Just as though the trees were burning.
While my berries split and show
Orange-coloured seeds aglow,
One by one my leaves must fall:
Soon the wind will take them all.
Soon must fairies shut their eyes
For the Winter's hushabies;
But, before the Autumn goes,
Spindle turns to flame and rose!

The Spindle Berry Fairy

THE SONG OF
THE HAZEL-NUT FAIRY

Slowly, slowly, growing
    While I watched them well,
See, my nuts have ripened;
    Now I've news to tell.
I will tell the Squirrel,
    " Here's a store for you;
But, kind Sir, remember
    The Nuthatch likes them too."

I will tell the Nuthatch,
    " Now, Sir, you may come;
Choose your nuts and crack them,
    But leave the children some."
I will tell the children,
    " You may take your share;
Come and fill your pockets,
    But leave a few to spare."

The Hazel-Nut Fairy

THE SONG OF
THE WHITE BRYONY FAIRY

Have you seen at Autumn-time
    Fairy-folk adorning
All the hedge with necklaces,
    Early in the morning?
Green beads and red beads
    Threaded on a vine:
Is there any handiwork
    Prettier than mine?

(This Bryony has other names—White Vine, Wild Vine, and
Red-berried Bryony. It has tendrils to climb with, which
Black Bryony has not, and its leaves and berries are quite
different. They say its root is white as the other's is black.)

The White Bryony Fairy

THE SONG OF
THE BEECHNUT FAIRY

O the great and happy Beech,
  Glorious and tall!
Changing with the changing months,
  Lovely in them all:

Lovely in the leafless time,
  Lovelier in green;
Loveliest with golden leaves
  And the sky between,

When the nuts are falling fast,
  Thrown by little me—
Tiny things to patter down
  From a forest tree!

(You may eat these.)

The Beechnut Fairy

THE SONG OF
THE HAWTHORN FAIRY

These thorny branches bore the May
   So many months ago,
That when the scattered petals lay
   Like drifts of fallen snow,
" This is the story's end," you said;
   But O, not half was told!
For see, my haws are here instead,
And hungry birdies shall be fed
   On these when days are cold.

The Hawthorn Fairy

THE SONG OF
THE PRIVET FAIRY

Here in the wayside hedge I stand,
And look across the open land;
Rejoicing thus, unclipped and free,
I think how you must envy me,
O garden Privet, prim and neat,
With tidy gravel at your feet!

(In early summer the Privet has spikes of very strongly scented
white flowers.)

The Privet Fairy

THE SONG OF
THE SLOE FAIRY

When Blackthorn blossoms leap to sight,
They deck the hedge with starry light,
  In early Spring
  When rough winds blow,
  Each promising
  A purple sloe.

And now is Autumn here, and lo,
The Blackthorn bears the purple sloe!
  But ah, how much
  Too sharp these plums,
  Until the touch
  Of Winter comes!

(The sloe is a wild plum. One bite will set your teeth on edge
until it has been mellowed by frost; but it is not poisonous.)

The Sloe Fairy

THE SONG OF
THE OLD-MAN'S-BEARD FAIRY

This is where the little elves
Cuddle down to hide themselves;
Into fluffy beds they creep,
Say good-night, and go to sleep.

(Old-Man's-Beard is Wild Clematis; its flowers are called
Traveller's Joy. This silky fluff belongs to the seeds.)

The Old-Man's-Beard Fairy

THE SONG OF
THE HOLLY FAIRY

O, I am green in Winter-time,
  When other trees are brown;
Of all the trees (so saith the rhyme)
  The holly bears the crown.
December days are drawing near
  When I shall come to town,
And carol-boys go singing clear
Of all the trees (O hush and hear!)
  The holly bears the crown!

For who so well-beloved and merry
As the scarlet Holly Berry?

The Holly Fairy